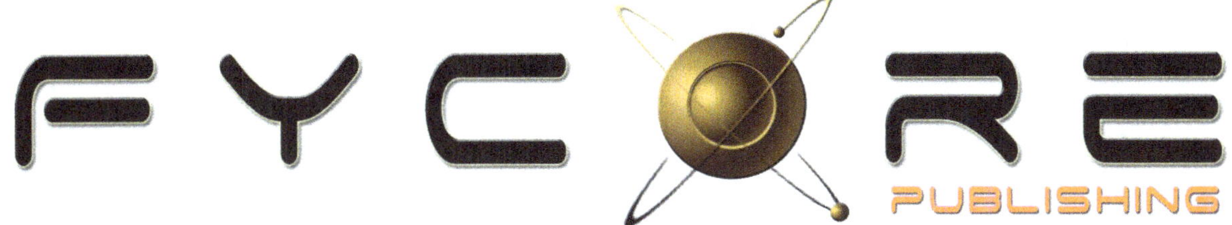

"THE HUMMING BEE"

Author: Victoria E. Kain
Book Contributors: Arnell Lane Hall | Development Editor: Jane Armstrong
Layout & Design by: | gritography.com | Illustrators Davis, Taylor E. Venegas
Publisher: Fycore Publishing | Subsidiary: Gritanium LLC
www.fycore.com

International Publisher Author Number: 1401425503240

International Standard Book Number: 9781619100022

Library of Congress Control Number: 2014930202

THE HUMMING BEE

"The Humming Bee" available soon in these additional formats:

CD (Audio Book)	$14.95	|	Hard Back	$19.95
MP3 (Audio Book)	$10.95	|	Soft Back	$12.95
PDF Book	$8.95	|	eBook	$9.95

For Inquiries:

131 Sunset Ave Ste E#353
Suisun City CA, 94585
Office | (800) 470-FYCORE
Facsimile: | (800) 531-0190
Web: | www.fycore.com

THE HUMMING BEE

Author: Victoria E. Kain

Once there was a happy little Honey Bee named Byrum who lived on Bee Hive Lane in the old Hickory Tree forest with his mother, and father and two brothers. Byrum was the oldest and was named after his grandfather who he loved very much but he did not like his name. He thought his name was too old for him and when he went to school the other honey bees would tease him.... Everyday Byrum would come home sad. His mother would say Byrum, you are a beautiful honey Bee and you should be happy you have your grandfather's name. Yes, Ma'am Byrum would say respectfully, as he had been taught to be polite to everyone. Every summer Byrum's family would visit their grandparents across the ocean. He often enjoyed the trip but was afraid to cross the ocean alone. He felt safe doing so with his parents, but knew that some day he would have to cross the ocean alone as all the young honey bees did when they grew up, but for now, he could not wait to see his grandfather and mother and was glad to travel with them. Grandpa always had good stories to tell them. He could not wait to hear the story! They all packed their honey and took off for their grandparent's home. Very soon they arrived at the old home hive where his grandparents had lived forever. Grandpa and grandma met them at the entrance of the hive and gave them big hugs! "We couldn't wait to get here Byrum said." I could not wait until you got here grandpa said. They all laughed, played and then hurried and ate their supper....they knew that when grandpa Byrum went to his old creeking rocking chair, he was about to tell them a story. They hurried and sat Down next to him and pleaded, please tell us a story grandpa...alright grandpa Byrum said...settle Down and I will tell you a story about a beautiful honey bee who was not happy with who he was.... Well, the story goes like this. "Once there was a beautiful island in the middle of the deep blue sea called "Ukeepaway" which was protected by mysteriously giant trees that were called, Limbastic trees. This island was said to be one of the most beautiful islands in the whole wide world. The way the island came into existence was during a terrible rain storm...one very cold winter night.

It was one of the worst storms in the oceans history. On that stormy night, the winds were so strong and the waves were high enough to reach the clouds in the sky! Each day the rain kept crashing down on the ocean floor raging and dashing in mid air with no place to go. The storm was so violent that it frightened all the animals from the surrounding shores and even the birds left the area. It washed everything away for miles and miles. When the storm was finally over, there was nothing left in its place. There was no dry land for any of the birds to land and rest from their travels. Days after the storm ended, a mysterious group of trees begin to grow out of the middle of the ocean floor. Every day the trees grew bigger and bigger, taller, and stronger. The leaves were dark green and very beautiful to look at! With each day that came and went, the trees became taller and taller until the entire ocean floor was covered with beautiful giant trees that could be seen for miles around. They had limbs that were long and strong and could reach through the clouds and swayed back and forth bringing a cool breeze during the hottest part of the day and shielding its inhabitants at night. The eagles and other flying creatures began to come back and fly high above the trees and would come and perch on the outstretched limbs of these trees because they felt safe to do so. The animals and birds began to appreciate the protection from predators inside the "Limbastic" trees. Finally the birds could feast on the morsels other birds would drop as they flew overhead and nothing could harm them. Some birds and squirrels would make their nest in the tall trees and some would simply rest for a while and fly on to their homes for the winter. "Yes, the Limbastic trees on Ukeepaway Island became their safe home. The trees would continue to grow as more and more animals began to come into Ukeepaway Island. Eventually everything that was within the Limbastic trees and their trunks, was a hiding place for all the critters. Over time, the beautiful trees had created a floor on the ocean and water could no longer come in because the Limbastic tree roots were so strong. After a while, nothing could be seen from outside of the trees by anyone by air or by boats that would sail by. Even though people were not able to live on Ukeepaway Island, they heard stories about it but as hard as they tried, they could never find the island. When ships passed by during a storm near Ukeepaway, they would dock outside of the mysteriously large trees for shelter until the storm passed over. The trees provided safety for those who came near the outside of them and those that lived on the inside of the island. The animals could live on Ukeepaway forever but there was a special rule that was created by the old "Mr. Hoot," the caretaker of the island. None of the animals, birds, fish or fowl could ever wish to be like any of the other animals from a different species. If they did, they would have to leave their happy home. Time stood still for the animals that lived on Ukeepaway Island. None of the animals would grow old or get sick…they could live there forever and ever. When there were little animals born, the parents of these animals would tell the little ones stories about how the island became invisible to people that lived on the other side of the ocean and only the animals could see how to get into "Ukeepaway!" How wonderful it was for each animal to know that Ukeepaway was just for them! The animals that came to Ukeepaway Island knew that people were never satisfied with who they were or with what they had. They always wanted to make changes to everything until it was no longer useful or sometimes things were destroyed in the process. When humans made changes to things, many times it would leave the animals without a home. On Ukeepaway Island the animals always had a home and food to eat. If you were a duck, you were always a duck. Beaks and feathers, and webbed feet and all…why, you even had your own special "Quack!" If you were a tiger, you were always a tiger. Your roar was not like any other tiger's at all. If you were a cat you were always a cat. A duck could not be a tiger. A tiger could not be a lion or a cat could not be a rat. Even the fish were unique and would swim in under the Limbastic roots with a narrow opening that only certain fish could find their way in by way of the

Forest streams. They would sing, *"Up the river and down the sea - Until we reach our destiny - We know there are no guarantees - Until we reach the Limbastic trees!"* The fish would sing this song until they reached the entrance of the roots of the Limbastic trees. There, they would swim inside. The doves would come in and roost on the limbs with the eagles. Everything that grew within the trees was beautiful and perfect.

Different animals would come onto the island until it was filled. Mr. Hoot, the owl had been on Ukeepaway from the very beginning. As the overseer of the Island he made sure that no one came into the forest without being announced as it was proper to do so. All of the animals, insects, birds, fish and fowl knew each other and they were never jealous of one another. This was the one thing that kept the peace and harmony among the animals on the island and helped them to live as one happy family. If you were an eagle, you could fly for miles on the island and never get tired and find the highest branch to perch on. The eagle's strong wings would never grow weak or tired. Even the bald eagle could grow hair on his beautiful head. The rabbits were plentiful and playful. No rabbit stew for these island inhabitants. The tigers and bears lived together and did not hunt each other but played all day in the sun. The monkeys had all the bananas they could eat and shared them with the gorillas and all the flying creatures were drawn to the island for safety.

Beautiful flowers and trees captivated the sun by day and by night the moon glistened off the clear blue water and lulled the animals to sleep…"Aaaaaaah, who would want to leave Ukeepaway Island… Not I "said Stundus the bear," as he rolled over in his cave…..Zzzzzzzz! When it rained, the rain would fall from the sky in very big drops. Sometimes, the rain drops were so big, each drop looked like giant water balloons falling from the sky bursting into huge puddles on the forest floor. But these rain drops never harmed any of the animals or plants like before when there were rain floods. This was because by the time the rain drops reached the forest floor they would fall ever so gently on the leaves of the Limbastic trees and the trees would gracefully bow low together to create an umbrella to protect the little creatures from losing their homes to a natural disaster from the flood waters. They would position their limbs together to make a gutter spout and the water would run right back out into the ocean. The plants would receive only the water needed to keep growing for a perfect balance. When the rain stopped, all the little creatures on the ground and in the trees would say… "Thank you Limbastic trees," the ants would say… in their tiny voices, "thank you, Limbastic trees, we love you…the snails would say. "Thank you Limbastic trees, we love you too? The Limbastic trees would bow low to the ground and wave their limbs in acceptance of the gratitude from the animals on the island. They enjoyed protecting the plants and animals. The Limbastic trees only allowed just the right amount of sun to come through to the forest to keep the plants, flowers and animals in perfect condition. Here on the island of Ukeepaway even the trees were happy! When the bright yellow sun would peek out from behind the clouds, shining down a big smile and warming the ground just enough to dry up all the extra water so the little spiders and bugs could come out again to play. “Ah, yes, said the piglets”, we are happy here on the beautiful Ukeepaway Island...everything is good . They all danced around in the warm sunlight and were happy! No one was afraid until one day... the alarm was sounded in the forest by Mr. Hoot. All the animals stopped in their TRACKS! They all saw something strange flying towards the island..." what could it be, growled the timid tiger?" What could it be, squeaked the tiny mouse?" What could it be...roared the lion with his furry mane. Everyone wanted to know what the noise was they heard. They understood that there was one of "every" kind of animal already in the forest... What they did not know was that there were "two" creatures left to complete their number. Could this noise be the last animal to enter the Ukeepaway forest...? They would soon find out. All the animals asked Mr. Hoot, "what is the animal that must come into the forest," and he said, "It was said that the

Island must have two more creatures...the only way we will know who they are is when the Limbastic trees permit them to come in. They all stood quietly and listened and looked intently in the middle of the forest to wait for the clock tower in the garden to strike at twelve noon. Finally when the clock struck 12 noon, and the sun was facing the north and the shadow of the water was shining on the island and made it easy for the new creatures to see their way into the dense forest, Mr. Hoot announced that the creature coming in matched exactly what was needed for Ukeepaway Island. At that point, all the animals scurried down to the entrance of the forest to welcome their new friend.

Mr. Bully Catt pranced hurriedly down the trail with his

feline Calico. Ringo, the tiger, growled as he scurried down with Dr. Meowski the island physician. The fire fly sisters, "Hither, Thither and Yond" flittered playfully high above Mr., Hoots head as they also hurried to see the new face in the forest. They all could not wait to see who would complete their forest home! Once all the inhabitants reached the entrance of the forest. They sat quietly looking up at the tall trees and waited for their new friends to arrive. At first it sounded like a plane engine..."buzzzzzzzzz buzzzzzzzzz, buzzzzzzzz." The sound was getting louder and louder! It was a very fast sound but was also like a whisper at the same time. "What could it be, they thought... It sounded as if someone was fanning out the flames of a large fire. The animals had never heard this sound before and had no idea what it could be. Many of the animals were becoming afraid for the first time. They began to back up from the entrance of the forest not knowing what they would see. Finally...after a long pause, The whispering buzzing noise came closer and closer, and it sounded like a giant locust about to land on the island until finally....in plops a tiny humming bird. They all gasped at the tiny body and were surprised at how much noise it actually made the closer it got to the forest door! Swiftly fluttering his wings it flitters into the forest. To everyone's amazement, he was the tiniest little thing to be making such a noise, but they realized that the closer he got to the forest, the quieter he became and finally they could barely hear his wings flutter at all. They all cheered "Welcome home!" The strange noise from the welcoming animals startled the Hummingbird as he instinctively tried to turn around and fly out of the forest....but, the Limbastic trees softly put their branches together and closed the opening of the island and the hummingbird flew back into the forest. Mr. Hoot greeted the Hummingbird and asked, "What is your name son?" The tiny bird stated, "Horatio" sir, in a polite way, for Horatio was very "humble." He apologized for the intrusion and told Mr. Hoot he had gotten lost on his journey trying to find a new home, but he would be on his way home if he could show him the way out. Mr.

Hoot said to Horatio, "make yourself at home" my son, which he called all the animals that came into the forest. I will introduce you to the other animals. Horatio, liked Mr. Hoot's kind voice. So Horatio did what Mr. Hoot asked him to do. He smiled and greeted each of the animals. One by one. Horatio was a little reluctant coming up to animals that might normally try to harm him outside the forest, but Mr. Hoot assured Horatio with the wide eyed look that no one in the forest would ever harm him. He began to feel safe and could see the entire beautiful forest as if his eyes were opened for the first time. When Horatio was no longer afraid, he was able to see a garden of flowers and plants that would take him years to pollinate.

This was truly a beautiful place! It was like nothing he had ever seen before. Horatio, began to feel happy and after meeting all the other animals, he would go from one beautiful flower to the next until he became intoxicated with the beauty of the island. The nectar was sweeter than any he had ever tasted and he didn't realize that time was flying by quickly. He enjoyed watching all the animals in the forest have fun with each other and smiled and danced in the air. His wings were fluttering hundreds of miles per minute. After a while, he wanted to have fun too! Horatio watched the butterflies group together and flitter around the island with their colorful array of designs on their wings. The fire flies went by and they all laughed and enjoyed themselves as they waved and blinked their tails that lit up as they went by. Horatio, smiled and was having fun watching everyone else have fun realizing he had no one to fly with him. Finally Horatio sat down with his wings still fluttering and looked in the pool of water by the base of the old Limbastic tree and wished that he had a friend too. He wanted someone that understood what he liked to do as a Hummingbird, which was pollinating flowers. Just when he had wished he had a friend. Mr. Hoot was once again perched at the entrance of the forest and sounded the alarm! To everyone's, even Horatio, who had just arrived, realized another was about to enter the forest on the same day! The animals heard another buzzing sound coming from the ocean but this time the sound was heavier than the first. All of the animals stopped to listen as the sound got closer and closer. At first Artez the alligator said…"what is that sound" I have never heard that before? It sounds like a motor cycle. Artez use to be in the circus and remember that sound of the motor cycle. What can it be? They all began to wonder what it was and even Horatio turned to look with all of his new found friends. Finally…"the buzzing became unbearable and they all hid behind the Limbastic trees. It took a few minutes and finally, in drops a colorful Happy Honeybee with boots dangling from his rosy legs. He had bright red hair and brown boots with a black coat of fur and a yellow belly. After the honeybee came into the forest Mr. Hoot asked the Honey Bee's name and he said "It's Byrum, and smiled and hurried along to the first flower! He immediately saw the beautiful flowers and plants and did not wait for any introductions but immediately begin to see the beautiful flowers and hurried to them. Horatio, decided to flit over and flew up to Byrum as he was pollinating the flowers. Horatio playfully followed him. Each flower Byrum went to, Horatio went to also. Finally Byrum was so gorged with nectar he had to sit down on a flower pedal. Horatio began to flutter around and around the flower as Byrum sat there moaning….."ooooh, I am too full he said…I have to sit for a while. Horatio flitted around playfully and asked

Byrum if he wanted to race to see who could get to the next flower the fastest. Horatio told Byrum if he was too full from the nectar he needed to get up and move around and it would make him feel better. Byrum didn't like having to move when he was full of nectar but Horatio kept insisting it would make him feel better so Byrum finally agreed and slowly got up and begin to race towards the next group of beautiful flowers. Each time they both reached the flower, they laughed and began to talk about how great the other one was. "Your wings are very fast, "said Byrum. Horatio said, I know! They are always fast and I can keep going and going ...watch what I can do" said Horatio." Horatio, the hummingbird flew in circles to impress his new found friend. Byrum the honey bee looked on in amazement as he went to the next flower. "I like the way you go from flower to flower and collect all the nectar with your long beak, "said Byrum." And your legs do not get full of the nectar like mine do either..." Byrum looking sad now because of all the things that Horatio could do. Byrum stops and stomps off the excess pollen from his furry legs. Horatio now realizes that his new friend is sad and wants to say something to make him feel better so he said, "I collect the nectar in my beak," said Horatio, but Byrum, your legs are covered in pollen...that is so cool, "said Horatio." Awww, that's nothing, "said Byrum," feeling better that his friend has complimented him. I can take a lot of pollen with me to pollinate the flowers, said Byrum, ... when I was little my brothers use to collect more than me, but now, I can collect more than them. I wish they could be here to see what I can do now. Finally feeling more confident, Byrum told Horatio, “watch what I can do” and speedily goes from flower to flower until his legs are so full of pollen he has to stop again. Byrum stops and begins to shake the pollen off his legs. They both look at each other and laugh! They are very happy as new friends! The flowers all smile and chant, “thank you Byrum” we hope you stay in the forest. Byrum and Horatio talk about what they like about each other. Not understanding the rules Mr. Hoot had given them when they entered Ukeepaway island , Horatio begins to say,

“I wish I were a Humming Bird” said Byrum. No, said Horatio I wish I were a Honey Bee. After saying those words…something strange happened! They looked around the forest and realized that all the laughter and noise had stopped! What just happened, asked Byrum?” I don’t know” said Horatio. The wind began to blow very briskly, and the Limbastic tree limbs bowed low to the ground and in fly’s ole Mr. Hoot. Mr. Hoot, perched on the tallest tree and looks down at the two new best friends Byrum the Honey Bee and Horatio the hummingbird. At this time, Mr. Hoot, says to them, it is time for the two of you to leave the forest. Byrum and Horatio both spoke at the same time…”but we don’t want to leave,“ they both said! ”We like it here Mr.

Hoot." Did we do something wrong? Mr. Hoot told them again about the only rule to living on Ukeepaway Island. He explained that all of the animals had to be satisfied with who they are. They cannot want to be like anyone else on the island, because they were all special in their own way. Byrum and Horatio were very sad. Mr. Hoot further said, there is one other thing, they both asked, "what is that, Mr. Hoot?" Mr. Hoot stated...you have only one day to decide if this is where you want to live forever. Mr. Hoot tells them again that it is time to leave the island and this time, he escorts them to the entrance of the forest where they came in. The Limbastic trees open their limbs wide and let the two best friends out. Byrum and Horatio are happy that they are best friends but sad because they must leave. As they begin to fly out beyond the trees Mr. Hoot tells them not to be one minute late if they are to return to the island or it will be closed forever to them. Mr. Hoot, also, tells them there was something they had to do before they could come back as well. They did not know what he meant, but Horatio and Byrum said their goodbyes and thanked Mr. Hoot for his hospitality. The two new best friends promised to meet back at the forest the next day. They agreed that they would figure out what they needed to know in order to live on Ukeepaway Island. They waved goodbye and went to their separate homes. As they got further and further away from Ukeepaway forest, they began to feel afraid again... they remembered that in the forest they had no fear. They hurried home to get there before dark. When Byrum arrived home, he was excited and told his parents about his adventure for the day and told them about Mr. Hoot the owl and Hoppy the kangaroo and Hither Thither and Yond the fireflies and even the Limbastic trees. His parents listened but they did not understand much of what he was saying. On the other side of the woods Horatio told his parents about his adventure and Mr. Hoot and Hither Thither and Yond and the Limbastic trees and his parents did not understand much either. They both ate their dinner and went to bed early only to have a strange dream. That night...a very strange thing happened. As they both slept, in their own beds in separate places, they had the same dream. In the dream, Horatio and Byrum dreamed that they became like the other one. They both said in the forest that they wanted to be like each other but in the dream they had not switched places with each other but had been 'COMBINED INTO ONE HUMMING BEE! Horatio's body was too heavy and Byrum's wings were too light to carry him. In their dream they laughed and thought it was great, but when they saw how they looked and they tried to fly, they realized they could not go fast enough anymore. Byrum thought that if he had Horatio's wings he could fly longer because humming bird wings never stop. Horatio thought that if he had the honey bees body he could hold more nectar in his beak and in his bee legs but they were too short for him. They thought it would be cool to be like the other one, but it was not. They no longer could pollinate the flowers. They also could not fly as fast or stay out as long in the sun or even fly around and play like they did when they were themselves. The plants and flowers were not able to be pollinated and they began to disappear which made the forest look very sad. Trying to be like each other did not make them happy at all and they finally realized that it was no fun at all being like each other. In the dream they tried to make the flowers and plants grow but they no longer had the ability to do so. With no pollen nothing would grow and everything withered up in the forest. Horatio and Byrum were now very sad. They finally came to the Lilly pond and sat next to Lilly and marigold the two flowers. Lilly and marigold said, "We are sad because all of the animals must leave because the plants are drying up. We liked you the way you were and they began to cry… Don't cry Lilly and marigold "said Byrum and Horatio." Maybe it will be better tomorrow. They both realized what Mr. Hoot said, they went to the water fall and looked and saw their reflection in the water and they both had tears in their eyes… " They did not look the same and they were sad! Maybe tomorrow it will be better. Finally, they realized the mistake they had made by wanting to be something they were not. The Humming Bird said in his heart, "I thought I wanted to be a honeybee, but my wings are too light and I must keep moving. My body is too heavy for my wings to flutter all day and night. I am exhausted said Horatio! They both wished they could go back to the way they were. As they sat on the side of the water fall, gazing at the reflection of what had become, tears fell from their eyes and made ripples in the water, it caused them to become drowsy, until they were sound asleep. "Cock-a-doodle-doo," said the old rooster who crowed loudly from next door. Horatio and Byrum woke up from their dreams. It was finally morning again...and Byrum the honeybee jumped up and flew out of the bee hive to see if he looked like his friend the hummingbird and he realized he did not. "Yippee, he said out loud!" He was himself again, a happy red haired honey bee... he jumped for joy and hurried down for breakfast. Horatio, the humming bird awakened on the opposite side of town as well and quickly flittered around his nest high in the tree top and realized that it was only a dream! He too was very happy and flew down for breakfast and ate faster than he ever eaten before. Horatio and Byrum could not wait to see each other again in the forest. They both now remembered what Mr. Hoot said and realized they only had a short time to get back to the forest before their time was up! They both said their final goodbyes to their family and met up at the edge of the ocean. They flew for a long time and talked on the way back to Ukeepaway Island. They both realized what Mr. Hoot had warned them about right before they reached the entrance to the forest. They finally made it back to the area where they thought they came to the entrance of Ukeepaway Island before, but neither of them could see the forest! They became afraid that they would never get back in. Suddenly when they looked at each other with sad eyes, and said, "If we cannot go back to the forest, I am happy with the way I am," said Horatio. Me too, said Byrum. I am happy being a Honey Bee! Just then, they looked ahead of them and there it was, they were no longer afraid and had learned their lesson. They could now see the Limbastic trees waving them into the forest. Byrum and Horatio, smiled a big smile and flew side by side into the forest. All the creatures cheered for them as they were about to enter Ukeepaway forest for the last time. They were greeted by their new friends and the forest looked more beautiful than it did the first time. As the clock struck 12 noon in the forest, Horatio the Humble Hummingbird and Byrum the Happy Honeybee, were to become the final two creatures to join the Ukeepaway forest family never to look back or talk about wanting to be like each other again. The Limbastic trees stretched open their majestic limbs to the entrance of the Ukeepaway forest.

They would protect the forest and keep the animals safe as they enjoyed their happy life with their new family. Each of them would always be happy with who they are and live forever on Ukeepaway Island.

~To be continued~

Coming Soon

The Humming Bee
The Great Storm

(Book 2 of 7)

If you purchased any book from the Humming Bee Series, you are considered a fan, and that entitles you to special offers. You may pre order an early release copy of the next book from the series to release 12/2014 (2 of 7), and obtain keepsake merchandise that will be available for a limited time. Be the first to pre order your next copy up to 2 months before it releases. The next book will be beautifully illustrated in color and have a very exciting continuation of this story where all of the characters will come to life!

A message from old Mr. Hoot.

With your purchase of **The Humming Bee,** *Byrum the Honey Bee will send you a* **"Be Happy With Who You Are"** *Limited Edition 11x17 poster that features any one of your favorite selected characters. Your poster will also include your name and be autographed with a special message to you all for only $5.*

Pre Order Today!

For more information visit

www.thehummingbee.com

www.ingramcontent.com/pod-product-compliance
Lightning Source LLC
Chambersburg PA
CBHW080812020826
48982CB00017B/938
* 9 7 8 1 6 1 9 1 0 0 0 2 2 *